CHILDREN'S FAVORITE POEMS AND SONGS

# Five Little Monkeys

[redacted]

Distributed by The Child's World®
1980 Lookout Drive • Mankato, MN 56003-1705
800-599-READ • www.childsworld.com

Acknowledgments
The Child's World®: Mary Berendes, Publishing Director
The Design Lab: Kathleen Petelinsek, Design and Page Production



Library of Congress Cataloging-in-Publication Data
Avril, Lynne, 1951–
Five little monkeys / illustrated by Lynne Avril.
p. cm.
Summary: A counting book in which one by one the little monkeys jump on the bed only to fall off and bump their heads. End notes list the benefits of nursery rhymes.
ISBN 978-1-60253-530-5 (alk. paper)
1. Nursery rhymes. 2. Children's poetry. [1. Nursery rhymes. 2. Monkeys—Poetry. 3. Counting.] I. Title.
PZ8.3.A9378Fi 2010
398.8—dc22 2010015200

Printed in the United States of America in Mankato, Minnesota.
July 2010
F11538

ILLUSTRATED BY LYNNE AVRIL

Five little monkeys
jumping on the bed.

One fell off and
bumped his head.

Mama called the doctor,

and the doctor said,

"No more monkeys
jumping on the bed!"

# POEM ACTIVITY

**Say the poem five times. But each time, leave out the last line. With each repetition, take away one monkey.**

Five little monkeys jumping on the bed.
One fell off and bumped his head.
Mama called the doctor,
And the doctor said, . . .

(Four little monkeys jumping on the bed. . . . )
(Three little monkeys jumping on the bed. . . . )
(Two little monkeys jumping on the bed. . . . )

**When you are down to just one monkey, end the poem as follows:**

One little monkey jumping on the bed.
He fell off and bumped his head.
Mama called the doctor,
And the doctor said,
"No more monkeys jumping on the bed!"

# BENEFITS OF CHILDREN'S POEMS AND SONGS

**Children's poems and songs are more than just a fun way to pass the time. They are a rich source of intellectual, emotional, and physical development for a young child. Here are some of their benefits:**

- Learning the words and activities builds the child's self-confidence—"I can do it all by myself!"
- The repetitious movements, if any, build coordination and motor skills.
- The close physical interaction between adult and child reinforces both physical and emotional bonding.
- In a context of "fun," the child learns the art of listening in order to learn.
- Learning the words expands the child's vocabulary. He or she learns the names of objects and actions that are both familiar and new.
- Repeating the words helps develop the child's memory.
- Learning the words is an important step toward learning to read.
- Reciting the words gives the child a grasp of English grammar and how it works. This enhances the development of language skills.
- The rhythms and rhyming patterns sharpen listening skills and teach the child how poetry works. Eventually the child learns to put together his or her own simple rhyming words—"I made a poem!"

## ABOUT THE ILLUSTRATOR

Lynne Avril has two little monkeys of her own—her grandchildren—and they do like to jump on the bed! Lynne has illustrated over 60 books for children, including the *New York Times* Bestsellers *Amelia Bedelia's First Day of School* and *Amelia Bedelia's First Valentine*. Lynne lives in Phoenix, Arizona.

[redacted]